I feel Grateful for my day

SARA AND DÁMASO MEDINA

Dedication
This book is dedicated to all children. We, the authors, believe that parents or caregivers have a great opportunity to serve the world through them, our children. We dedicate this book to our oldest daughter. Thank you, girl, for inspiring us to become our best versions of ourselves. God bless you!

Written by Sara E Medina
Designed by Dámaso D Medina
Illustrated by Mauro Sánchez
Edited by Michelle Wanasundera
Proofread by Becky Ross Michael

THIS BOOK BELONGS TO

....

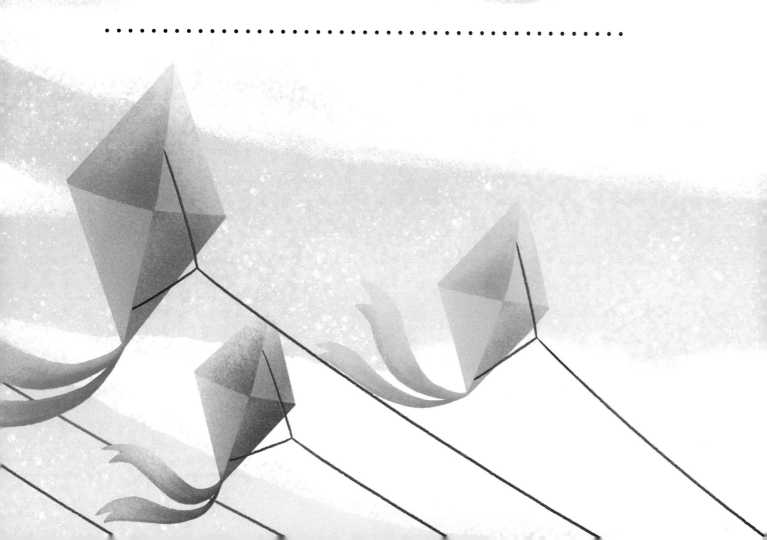

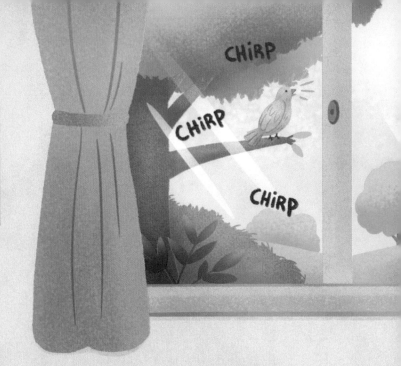

Each day I feel so grateful,
To open up my eyes,

With each day there is always,
A brand-new surprise.

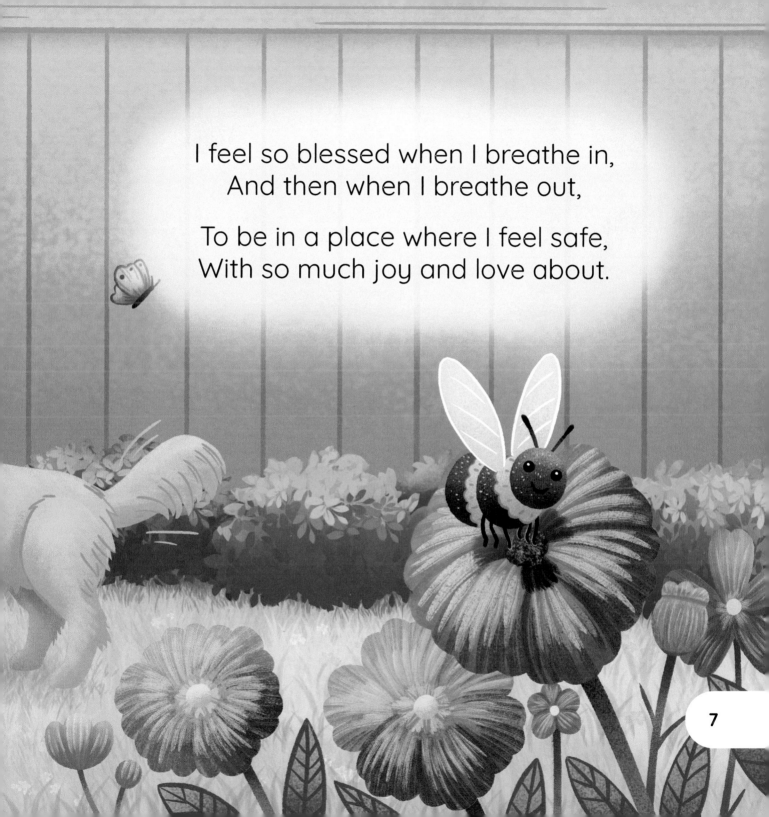

I feel so blessed when I breathe in,
And then when I breathe out,

To be in a place where I feel safe,
With so much joy and love about.

I get up, then clean my teeth,
Wash my face, and then run free,

I eat my breakfast, which always is so healthy and quite yummy.

I like to make it funny,
Whenever I start my day,

Oh, truly what a blessing
To learn and then to play.

Surrounded by my loved ones,
I dance and I sing songs,

I feel so free to be myself,
It's where my heart belongs.

I like to create stories,
Allowing my imagination to run free,

Because it also strengthens
All my creativity.

I kick a ball and climb a tree,
Which builds my motor skills,
The simple things like moving around,
Can give me happy thrills.

At noon it's lunchtime,
And first I bless my food,

Wow! I feel so lucky that
It really tastes so good!

I get ready for my afternoon,
Full of activities and chores to do,

Like sports, dancing, or finger painting,
And practice my ABCs too!

Then it's time to have a snack,
And I know I must clean my room,

Because it's become so messy,
By the end of the afternoon!

But OH, I have so much to do!
the list is long in my head,

I DON'T want to clean my room,
I'd much rather play instead!

I breathe in and breathe out, when
difficult feelings are about.

I sort my toys and stack my books,
With music on in the background!

It's so cool to tidy up my room,
While still singing and playing around!

COSTUMES

A M

G

And when the sun has set,
It's time to get some rest,

I eat my dinner and take a bath
Relaxing is just the best.

But then it is the time for bed!
The day is finished? Oh, nooo!

It can't be time for bed so soon,
I really DON'T want to go!

I breathe in and breathe out, when
difficult feelings are about.

I feel better and put my jammies on,

I brush my teeth, then hop into bed,

I have my friend, soft teddy bear,
He's such a sleepy head.

I'm going to bed with a good night kiss,
And I feel grateful for,

the joy and fun I've had today,
I couldn't wish for more.

Each night I feel so grateful,
To gently close my eyes,

Knowing that tomorrow will hold,
A brand-new surprise.

I feel grateful for... (Caregivers)

I feel grateful for... (Child)

Thank you note

We, the authors, are very grateful you took the time to read our work. We invite you to leave a review and tell other parents or caregivers about the book to help spread the word. We really hope this work can cultivate gratitude and mindfulness at home.

Thanks for supporting our work!

Blessings to you!

S&D :-)

Made in the USA
Las Vegas, NV
26 November 2023